ADAPTED BY
Teresa Mlawer

ILLUSTRATED BY
Olga Cuéllar

Little Red Riding Hood

D0818177

Once upon a time there was little girl who lived in a small house near the woods. Everyone called her Little Red Riding Hood because she always wore a red hooded cape that her grandmother had made for her.

One day, Little Red Riding Hood's mother told her that her grandmother was not feeling well.

She asked Little Red Riding Hood to go to her grandmother's house and take her a jar of honey and an apple pie that she had made.

Before she left, Little Red Riding Hood's mother reminded her to be careful in the woods. She was not to stop and talk to anyone so she could get to her grandmother's house quickly.

Little Red Riding Hood was happily walking in the woods, when suddenly, she came across a wolf that had not eaten in a long time.

"Little Red Riding Hood, where are you going with that beautiful red cape?" asked the wolf.

"I'm going to see my grandmother, who is not feeling well," said Little Red Riding Hood.

"What are you carrying in that basket?"

"I'm taking her an apple pie and a jar of honey to make her feel better."

"Does your grandmother live far?"

"No, she lives on the other side of the woods."

"I know a shortcut to her house," said the wolf.

"On the way, you'll find very pretty flowers and you can make a beautiful bouquet. That will surely make her happy."

"That's very nice of you, Mr. Wolf," said Little Red Riding Hood.

The wolf ran off so he could get to the grandmother's house before Little Red Riding Hood.

"Bang, bang," he knocked on the door.

"Who's there?" asked the grandmother from her bed.

"It's me, grandma," answered the wolf, imitating the voice of Little Red Riding Hood.

"Just push open the door, it's not locked," said the grandmother.

And before you could count to three,
the wolf went into the house and locked
the grandmother in the closet.

Then he put on her nightgown and
bonnet, slipped into bed, and covered
himself with the blanket.

A little while later, Little Red Riding Hood, holding a beautiful bouquet of flowers, knocked on the door.

"Come in, my dear granddaughter," said the wolf, imitating the grandmother's voice.

Little Red Riding Hood approached the bed. It seemed to her that her grandmother looked very different, but she thought it was because she was not feeling well.

She took a closer look at her and said:

"Grandma, what big arms you have!"

"The better to hug you with," said the wolf.

"Grandma, what big eyes you have!"

"The better to see you with, my dear granddaughter."

"Grandma, what big ears you have!"

"The better to hear you with, my darling."

"Grandma, what a big mouth you have!" cried
Little Red Riding Hood, who was now very frightened.

"The better to eat you with!" shouted
the wolf as he jumped out of bed to catch
Little Red Riding Hood.

But at that very moment, two hunters were passing by and heard Little Red Riding Hood's screams.

They rushed into the house, captured the wolf,
and took him far, far away into the woods.

And ever since that day, Little Red Riding Hood always remembered her mother's advice. She never again strayed from the path or stopped to talk to anyone on her way to visit her grandmother.

FOR INFORMATION, PLEASE CONTACT ADIRONDACK BOOKS, P.O. BOX 266, CANANDAIGUA, NEW YORK, 14424

ISBN 978-0-9883253-7-1   10 9 8 7 6 5 4 3 2   PRINTED IN CHINA